CHRISTOPHER PUMPKIN

For Wanda, who likes all things fun
S.H. & P.L.

For Jon E, a spooky goth at heart
N.E.

Hodder
Children's
Books

HODDER CHILDREN'S BOOKS

First published in Great Britain in 2019 by Hodder and Stoughton

Text © Sue Hendra and Paul Linnet 2019
Illustrations © Nick East 2019

A CIP catalogue record of this book
is available from the British Library.

HB ISBN: 978 1 444 93782 4
PB ISBN: 978 1 444 93094 8

10 9 8 7 6 5 4 3 2 1

Printed and bound in China.

MIX
Paper from
responsible sources
FSC® C104740
FSC
www.fsc.org

Hodder Children's Books
An imprint of
Hachette Children's Group
Part of Hodder and Stoughton
Carmelite House
50 Victoria Embankment
London EC4Y 0DZ

An Hachette UK Company
www.hachette.co.uk

www.hachettechildrens.co.uk

CHRISTOPHER PUMPKIN

Written by
Sue Hendra
and **Paul Linnet**

Illustrated by
Nick East

On Snaggletooth Lane in spooky Spooksville
was a dark creepy castle, perched high on a hill.

Deep in that castle, by the glow of the fire
sat a wicked old witch with a burning desire –
to throw a huge party, the scariest yet.
One that her friends would never forget.

SCARY
PARTY
TOMORROW

"There's too much to do! It'll drive me beserk!
Now who can I find that will do all the work?"

She looked all around – then what did she spy,
but a big pile of pumpkins she'd bought for a pie.

"THEY could be useful and scary as well.
I'll bring them to life with the help of a spell . . ."

She was making an army and having a ball.
As they sprang into life she gave names to them all.

"Gnarly,

Grizzly,

Grunty,

Roar,

Stink Face

Snaggletooth,

and maybe one more . . ."

The witch raised her wand for one final go.
There were SPARKLES and GLITTER then a voice said . . .

Hello!
I'm Christopher Pumpkin.
I like all things fun.
I'm SO happy to be here.
Group hug, everyone?

He stretched out his arms and gave them a grin,
and out shone the warmth and the kindness within.

"OH NO!" screeched the witch. "What on earth did I make?
You're supposed to be scary. I've made a mistake!"

"Now, hang on a minute," said Christopher P.
"I'm sure I'll fit in. Just wait and you'll see."

"All right," snapped the witch, "as there's so much to do, but, Christopher Pumpkin . . . I'll be watching you!"

FIZZZ CRACKLE

"Now get on with your work and make decorations.
I want horrible, ghastly, frightful creations."

"Did someone say decor? That's right up my street!
Forget about tricks and prepare for a treat!"

There was lifting and shifting and huffing and grunting,
but while others hung cobwebs, Chris hung up bunting!

Then along came the witch. "Work harder, buffoons!"
But instead of bat lanterns, Chris chose balloons!

The horrified pumpkins all scuttled away.
They needed to find party music to play.

"My favourite music is howling and screaming,"
said Gnarly the Pumpkin, his scary eyes gleaming.

"I'm sorry," said Chris, "but that sounds bizarre.
Let's all have a sing-song. I've brought my guitar."

Now for the food. It was time to begin,
so they stood round the cauldron, tossing things in.

GLUG GLUG

Firstly some ear wax, then hair from a yeti,
a poisonous bug and some mouldy spaghetti.

The result was rat pizza, all sprouting with hair
and stinky green cheese made from old underwear,

some hot curried slugs, fried spicy snakes . . .

. . . then in walked our Chris with some pink fairy cakes!

"This just isn't working! I think you'll agree,"
said the witch as she glared down at Christopher P.

"I've had quite enough. You're not part of this group.
If you can't be scary, I'll turn you to soup!

You've got till the morning. Have I made myself clear?"
Poor Christopher nodded, frozen with fear.

"I don't want to be soup, or a pie, or a flan.
I'll stay up all night and think of a plan.

I'm Christopher Pumpkin. I like all things fun.
But there must be a way I can scare everyone."

He worked through the night, never taking a break.
But the clock, it was ticking.
Soon the witch would awake!

The morning arrived and the pumpkins all stared at Christopher's bed. "He's gone!" they declared.

"I suppose that it's better he went without fuss. There was really no chance he could ever scare US!"

Along came the witch. "Now out of my way,
my guests are arriving. The party's today!"

So poor Chris had vanished, or so it would seem,
but then from outside came an almighty . . .

There were unicorns skipping, balloons on the door,
pink fluffy kittens and sparkles galore!

There were marshmallow puffs, piled up in mountains.
Strawberry milkshake was squirting from fountains.

"I'm Christopher Pumpkin. I like all things fun."
But before he could finish the witch shouted . . .

"Well, one thing's for sure . . . I scared **them** all right!"